THIS BOOK is

DEDICATED TO GARY AND OLIVE

(MISS LODGED)

For Edwin, with Thanks for his help,
and for DaVid, who is A Clever Cowboy

(ANGELA McALLISTER)

DK
Ink

DK Publishing, Inc.
95 Madison Avenue, New York, New York 10016
Visit us on the World Wide Web at http://www.dk.com

Text copyright © 1998 by Angela McAllister
Illustrations copyright © 1998 by Katherine Lodge

ISBN 0-7894-3491-1

Published simultaneously in Great Britain by Dorling Kindersley Ltd.,
9 Henrietta Street, London WC2E 8PS

Printed and bound in Singapore by Tien Wah Press
First American Edition, 1998
2 4 6 8 10 9 7 5 3

SPECIAL THANK YOU to

MAUREEN, BERNARD and JANE

THE CLEVER COWBOY

by
Angela
McAllister

Illustrated by
Katherine Lodge

A DK INK BOOK
DK PUBLISHING, INC.

Clever Cowboy was a CLEVER cowboy.

He could cook a dish of chili beans so hot that your socks would jump off and dive in the creek.

He could dance the yakety-yak so fast that sparks flew from his boot heels.

And he could hear a mean snake
dream of rattling
as it slept in
the shade of a cactus.

One day Clever Cowboy needed some rope and a haircut,
so he rode into Yippeeville and tied up his horse.

GENERAL STORE

Outside the general store
was a poster that said . . .

TODAY!
YIPPEEVILLE
PANCAKE
TOSSIN'
COMPETITION

1ST PRIZE

OLD NAN TUCKET'S
BEST TELESCOPE

CONTEST BEGINS 12 NOON

All around town, in secret places, folk were stirring up their special batters, hoping to win **the Prize.**

Fred Farmer added a pinch of birdseed to his mixture.

Miss Prissy, in the schoolhouse, stirred hers with a silver spoon.

At twelve noon all the frying pans
of Yippeeville were spit 'n' sizzling hot.
The judge was the judge,
and he fired his gun.
The pancake tossin' began.

The sheriff tossed his pancake high into the air.
It flew over the jailhouse roof and landed on the head
of Six-Shooter Sam, who was escaping out the back.
EVERYONE CHEERED!

JAIL

Miss Prissy's pancake sat prettily in the pan, as still as a teacher's pet. EVERYONE BOOED!

Fred Farmer tossed his pancake high above the big barn, and EVERYONE CHEERED AGAIN!

Next came Clever Cowboy.
He felt his lucky pebble in his pocket
and whispered low,
"Get me up when I'm down, get me
out when I'm stuck, give me rainbows
of happy and a pocketful of luck!"

and ...

UP

and ...

UP

and ...

UP

and ...

UP

Then he tossed his pancake

It didn't come down!
"We can't have a winner
with no pancake," said
the judge. "Try again,
cowboy." So Clever Cowboy
fried another pancake and
tossed it up, up, and up ... and ...

UP and ...

UP and ...

UP ...

And then ...

"Reckon I tossed that pancake so high it just stuck on the sun and put the lights out," said Clever.

"Well," said the judge, "you'd better figure out a way of peelin' it off or I'll have to send everyone to bed."

Clever had an idea. He bought . . .

a parasol

a ball of elastic

a hammer

ten eggs and a cow

FLOUR

a sack of flour

Then he made a . . .

giant elasticated-one-seater-frying-pan catapult

and mixed up a
barrel of batter. The folks of
Yippeeville watched and waited. . . .

But nothing happened next.
And then more nothing. And then nothing happened all over again.

"Look here, we ain't got all day—I mean all night, cowboy," said the judge. Clever had to come clean. "I can't go up, folks," he said. "Guess I'm afraid of heights!" The folks gasped. Who else could ride on that pancake?

Clever just stuck his hands deep in his pockets and kicked the dust.

"I'll go up!" said Six-Shooter Sam, leaping out of an escape tunnel nearby.

He jumped on the **giant** elasticated -one-seater -frying-pan c a t a p u l t .

'You don't get away that easily!' called the sheriff, pulling out his handcuffs. But Six-Shooter took hold of the lever and . . .

PˮTˊˊCˊˊHANGˆ

He catapulted into the afternoon night.

Everyone held their breath as Six-Shooter zipped between the stars.

"Howdy do!" he cried to the sleepy moon.
Then, with a whip of a stolen lasso,
he flipped off the prize-winning
pancake, and the sun came out.

"That brave man has saved the day! I reckon Six-Shooter deserves a pardon."

"Aw, it was just my lucky pebble," said Six-Shooter. "Gets me up when I'm down, gets me out when I'm stuck, gives me rainbows of happy and a pocketful of luck."

"Why, it's long-lost Kate!" cried Clever.

Woof!

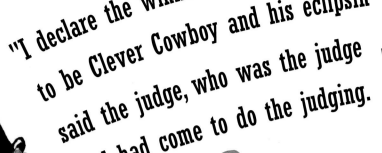

"I declare the winner of the pancake tossin' competition to be Clever Cowboy and his eclipsin' pancake!" said the judge, who was the judge and had come to do the judging. **EVERYONE**

Old Nan Tucket brought out her banjo, and Clever and Kate danced the yakety-yak so fast that sparks flew from their bucking boot heels. And then they danced some more!

CHEERED!